For Georgia, Isabel and Victoria
—JS

For Jane—howdy pardner!
—TW

tiger tales
an imprint of ME Media, LLC
202 Old Ridgefield Road, Wilton, CT 06897
Published in the United States 2004
Originally published in Great Britain 2004
By Little Tiger Press
An imprint of Magi Publications
Text copyright ©2004 Julie Sykes
Illustrations copyright ©2004 Tim Warnes
CIP data is available
ISBN 1-58925-041-9
Printed in Belgium

1 3 5 7 9 10 8 6 4 2

Bless You, Santa!

by **Julie Sykes**

Illustrated by
Tim Warnes

tiger tales

It was almost Christmas, and Santa was up very early one day.

"Jingle bells, jingle bells," he sang to himself. "Breakfast first and then to work."

He made some toast and took out the jam and butter. As he was pouring some cereal, though, his nose began to tickle.

"Aah, aah, aah . . ."

DECEMBER
23

"ACHOOOO!"

he roared. His sneeze blew
the cereal all over the place!

"Bless you, Santa," said Santa's cat, shaking
cereal out of her tail. "That's a nasty cold."
"Oh, no!" said Santa in alarm. "It can't be.
It's nearly Christmas. I don't have time for a cold."

After breakfast Santa rushed to his workshop and went to work on the unfinished toys. Happily he sang as he painted a robot. But Santa's sneezes were growing larger and louder.

"Aah, aah, aah . . ."

"ACHOOOo!"

"Bless you, Santa," squeaked Santa's little mouse, gathering the beads his sneeze had scattered across the table.

"Bless you, Santa," said Santa's cat, chasing paper stars as they fluttered around. "You sound awful. Go and sit by the fire."

"I feel awful," said Santa. "But I can't rest yet. It's too close to Christmas. I have to finish these toys or there will be no presents for all the . . . aah, aah, aah . . ."

"ACHOOOo!"

Santa sneezed so hard that he slipped and landed in a pile of balls. Down the balls tumbled, bouncing off Santa and bouncing around the room. They crashed into cars, they pushed over paint cans, they toppled the teddy bears, and they ruined the rockets.

"ACHOOOo!"

"Just look at this mess!" cried
Santa. "I'll never by ready in time
for Christmas."

"Go to bed, Santa," ordered his little mouse. "You're not well. Your nose is so red the reindeer could use it to guide your sleigh. We'll clean up this mess and get everything ready for Christmas."

So Santa's mouse put Santa to bed with a mug of hot tea and a little medicine to help his cold.

Santa snuggled into the blanket.

He sneezed. "ACHOOOO!"

He sniffled.

And finally he snored.

Meanwhile, back in the workshop, Santa's friends worked as hard as they could.
They mopped.

They mended.

They glued.

They snipped, they stuck, and they wrapped. Faster and faster they worked until every single present was finished. Then sleepily they went to bed.

The next evening, as the sun set, the animals waited with the sleigh piled high with toys.

"Where is Santa?" asked Santa's cat. "I hope he's better."

"Who's going to drive the sleigh and deliver all the presents?" asked the reindeer.

"Listen," said Santa's cat. "Can you hear something?"

The animals listened.

"It's Santa!" squeaked Santa's little
mouse. "Are you better, Santa? Can
you deliver the presents?"
Santa wrinkled his nose.
"Aah, aah, aah . . ."

"Only joking! I feel much better. Bless you, everyone. You did a great job! Thanks to you I will get these presents delivered in time for Christmas morning."

Santa climbed aboard his sleigh. "Reindeer, up, up, and away!" he shouted.

It was a busy night as Santa flew
around the world delivering presents.

When at last Santa landed back at the North Pole the sun was rising. But he hadn't finished quite yet.

"These presents are for you," said Santa.

"Presents for us?" squeaked Santa's cat. "Th . . . th . . . thaa . . ."

"ACHOOOo!"

Santa's cat sneezed so hard that a pile of snow fell off the trees and buried everyone. "Bless you!" laughed Santa. "And merry Christmas to you, too!"